SO-ELT-859

Tad Goes Shopping

Pre-Math

Learn numbers, counting and sorting
with Tad and his family.

"Here we are,
at the store!"
Mom says, "We'll buy
socks and more."

👂 "Like a fishing pole?"
asks Dad.
"And a teddy bear!"
says Tad.

GO

STOP

 "Aisle one, lots to do. Pens, pink paper, and white glue!"

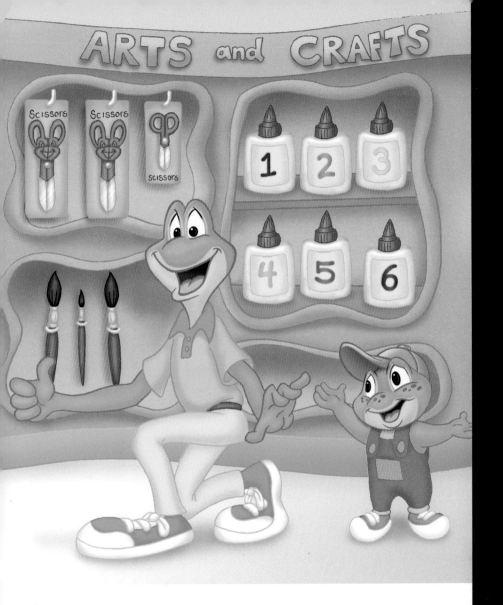

Tad asks with a happy smile, "Are there teddies in this aisle?"

 "Aisle two, lots to see. That's where fishing poles will be."

FISHING GEAR

2
FOR
1
SALE

"Let's get two for us!"
says Dad.
"What about my bear?"
asks Tad.

 "Aisle three, snacks to munch. Sandwiches with cheese for lunch."

Leap says, "Make mine three feet tall!" Tad asks, "Can you eat it all?"

"Aisle four, lots of fun. Shoes and socks for everyone."

SOCKS

👂 "Shoes in green and socks in blue. Striped and polka-dotted too!"

GO

 "Aisle five smells so sweet. Buying tulips is a treat!"

👂 "Flowers growing here and there." Tad asks, "Can I grow a bear?"

 "Aisle six, yummy yum! Lollipops and chewing gum."

"Candy pieces everywhere! Tad still wants a teddy bear."

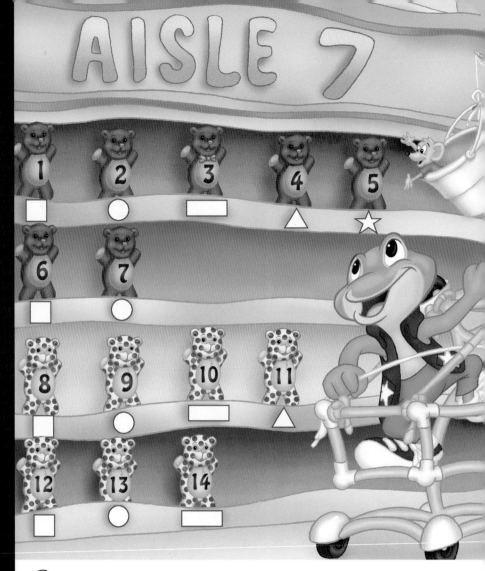

"One last aisle,
can you see?"
Tad says, "That's the
bear for me!"

 "Who can get it down from there?"

Leap says, "Tad, I'll get your bear!"

"Let's go home, now we're done. Shopping was a lot of fun!"
In the back seat, that is where, Tad's asleep with his new bear.